WE ARE
WOLVES

Molly Grooms & Lucia Guarnotta

For my pack, family and friends,
who have supported and inspired me.

$\mathcal{I}$t was a hot summer afternoon.
The wolf pack slept in the sun.

$\mathcal{A}$ crow landed with a flutter on a branch and woke two wolf cubs.
The crow and the cubs stared at each other with wide eyes.

*M*other Wolf called her cubs to her side.

"I am going hunting with the pack.

You two must stay here at the den with your uncle."

The little wolves cried, "No, no! We want to hunt!

We're big and brave! We will run fast and be quiet!"

Mother Wolf smiled and said, "Yes, you are big and brave. You can run fast and be quiet. But I need you to watch over Uncle Wolf and keep him out of trouble."

The little wolves sighed...

But Mother Wolf nuzzled them and licked their ticklish paws until they were giggling and happy again.

$\mathcal{E}$ach of the other wolves touched noses

with the cubs to say goodbye,

then trotted off to join the hunt.

The cubs watched as they

disappeared into

the woods.

LUCIA GUARNOTTA 1999

The cubs sat on the hill

watching them go.

Uncle Wolf could see they felt sad.

$\mathcal{H}$e picked up a feather and trotted past the cubs.

"Look what I have! This is a special feather that only big,

fast wolves can carry!"

And then he bounded away.

$\mathcal{T}$he cubs chased him, shouting,

"I want it, I want it!

I am a big, fast wolf! I am! I am!"

They caught Uncle Wolf and tumbled over him,

pulling his tail. The little wolves sat up laughing.

They said, "We can run faster than you, Uncle!"

"You may think you are grownup wolves,"

said Uncle, "but I am older and wiser.

I have been a wolf longer than you have.

Come with me for a walk, and I will show you."

$\mathcal{T}$hey trotted a short distance when

Uncle Wolf called, "Stop!"

The little wolves stood by him, puzzled.

"Look," said Uncle Wolf.

"Where, Uncle, where?" asked the cubs.

"Everywhere," Uncle said with a gentle smile.

The little wolves looked around, looking everywhere.

And they saw trees and birds and grass

moving in the wind.

"Look, look!" they cried. "Do you see those

yellow butterflies? And over there – that leaf is

moving like a wolf chasing its tail."

Uncle Wolf nodded. "Now you understand," he said.

"There is much to see in this world, little wolves.

Open your eyes and see the world.

That is what wolves do..."

"We are watchers."

"Now we will run!"

said Uncle Wolf as he began

to run as fast as he could through the woods.

He seemed to fly.

The cubs followed, running faster than they ever had

before. Their paws barely touched the ground.

It felt wonderful, and they laughed into the wind.

Uncle Wolf and the cubs stopped at the bank of a stream,

their hearts pounding. Between pants, the cubs asked,

"Can we do it again, Uncle?"

Uncle Wolf said, "Yes, another day. And soon, when you

are bigger, we will run faster and longer than today.

We will run all day and night and never get tired.

For that is what wolves do..."

"We are travelers."

Suddenly, Uncle Wolf said, "Shhhhh! Just listen."

The cubs listened harder than they ever had before.

And they heard more sounds than they thought the

world could hold. They heard woodpeckers knocking on

dead trees. They heard the stream gurgling over the stones.

Far away, they heard a squirrel rustling in the leaves.

"What do you hear?" asked Uncle Wolf.

"Oh, everything!" whispered the little wolves. "We hear so

many sounds!"

"There will always be more to hear," said Uncle Wolf.

"Learn to keep your ears awake at all times. A wise wolf is

a wolf who listens. For that is what wolves do."

"We are listeners."

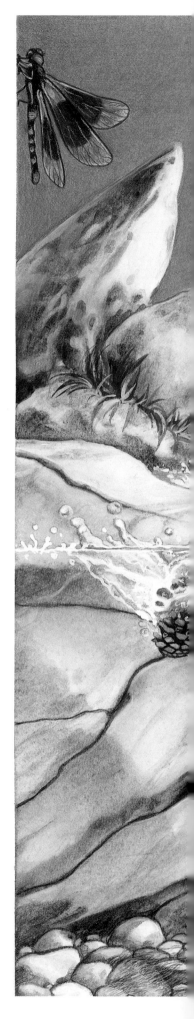

The little wolves sat beside their Uncle waiting for the next lesson. He was staring through the bubbly surface of the brook, watching a trout swimming left and right to catch insects.

"That fat trout would be good for lunch," said Uncle Wolf.

"Do you think you can catch it?"

The cubs leaned over the stream and held their breath. They gathered their courage, preparing to pounce.

"Be careful," whispered Uncle Wolf,

"or the trout will see you!"

𝒯oo late! The trout saw the little wolves and darted away in a flash of swirling water. The cubs were left looking at their own reflection.

"Be cautious when trying to get close to another animal," said Uncle Wolf. "Learn to walk on silent paws and stay close to the ground so you are almost invisible.

For that is what wolves do."

"We are hunters."

The cubs nodded and said, "Next time we will be more careful, Uncle Wolf."

Uncle Wolf smiled. "Yes, I think you will be better hunters. And you will run faster, see better and hear more."

Then the little wolves began to play in the grass.

They rolled and growled and jumped.

Just then, their ears pricked up. A sound floated through the woods to them. It was the pack, howling greetings as they returned home!

The little wolves raced to the den.

There, they found their mother and the rest of the pack greeting each other, sharing the news of the hunt. Then the whole pack sat down, turned their muzzles to the sky and howled. Uncle Wolf said with a smile,

"This is the song we sing when we come back together.

This is the song of the pack.

For that is what wolves are."

"We are family."

*L*ater that night, the two little wolves snuggled close to their mother. They started to tell her all that they had learned that day, but they were too sleepy to finish the story.

She smiled and licked their faces with long, loving strokes. And as they drifted off to sleep, she said, "Sleep now, my tired little wolves. Sleep in peace. I will watch over you and keep you safe.

For that is what wolves do, too."

"We are keepers."

 We are watchers.

 We are travelers.

 We are listeners.

 We are hunters.

 We are family.

 We are keepers.

"We are wolves."

© YOYO Books, Olen, Belgium

Cover design by Russell S. Kuepper

Library of Congress Cataloging-in-Publication Data
Grooms, Molly.
    We are wolves / text by Molly Grooms ; illustrations by Lucia Guarnotta.
        p.   cm.
    Summary: Two wolf cubs run with their uncle and make exciting discoveries
about what it means to be a wolf.
    ISBN 978-946033-984-4 (softcover)
    1. Wolves--Juvenile fiction.   [1. Wolves Fiction.]   I. Guarnotta,
Lucia, ill.   II. Title.
    PZ10.3.J93 Wg   1999
    [E]--dc21
                                00-028350

Printed in Singapore
10